UNDERWINTER

The Queen of Spirits

RAY FAWKES
Creator, Writer, Artist

STEVE WANDS
Letterer

"God made men / But he used a monkey to do it."

- DEVO

"We're not the Monkees / Hey Hey we're the Monkees"

- The KLF

image

UNDERWINTER: THE QUEEN OF SPIRITS TP. First printing. November 2018. Published by Image Comics, Inc. Office of publication: 2701 NW Vaughn St., Suite 780, Portland, OR 97210. ISBN: 978-1-5343-0866-4.

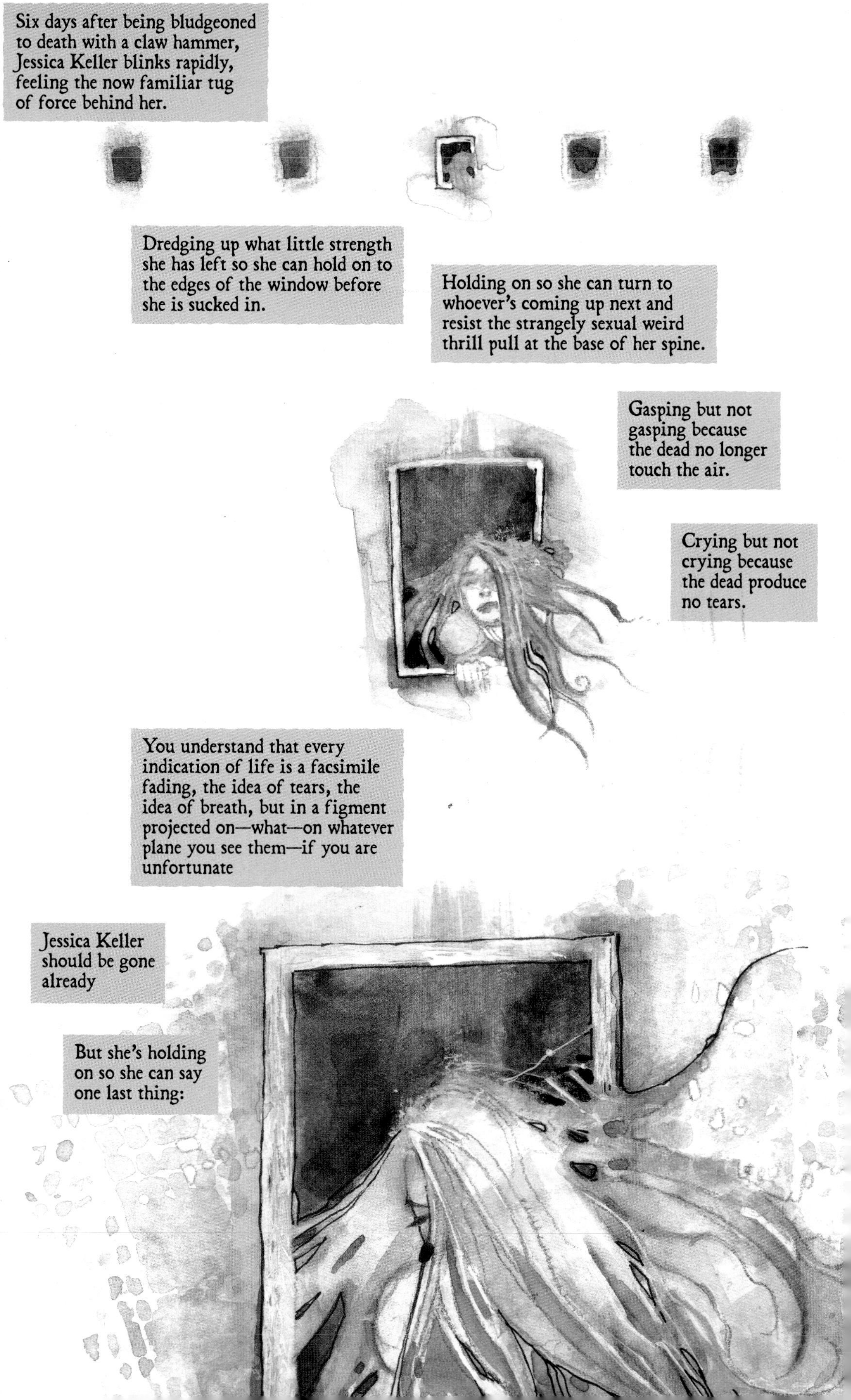
Six days after being bludgeoned to death with a claw hammer, Jessica Keller blinks rapidly, feeling the now familiar tug of force behind her.
Dredging up what little strength she has left so she can hold on to the edges of the window before she is sucked in.
Holding on so she can turn to whoever's coming up next and resist the strangely sexual weird thrill pull at the base of her spine.
Gasping but not gasping because the dead no longer touch the air.
Crying but not crying because the dead produce no tears.
You understand that every indication of life is a facsimile fading, the idea of tears, the idea of breath, but in a figment projected on—what—on whatever plane you see them—if you are unfortunate
Jessica Keller should be gone already
But she's holding on so she can say one last thing:

PLEASE. LISTEN TO ME. SHE'S REAL. EVERYTHING THEY TOLD ME IS TRUE.
SHE'S REAL AND SHE'S RIGHT IN HERE AND OH GOD, IT'S INCREDIBLE. I'LL HAVE THAT CHANCE. IF YOU BELIEVED IN HER, YOU WERE RIGHT.
IF YOU DIDN'T IT'S NOT TOO LATE.
I'M GOING TO LET GO NOW. YOU'RE SO LUCKY. I NEVER--I NEVER DID CATCH YOUR NAME.
YOU'LL SEE. SOON YOU'LL SEE.
JUST REMEMBER:

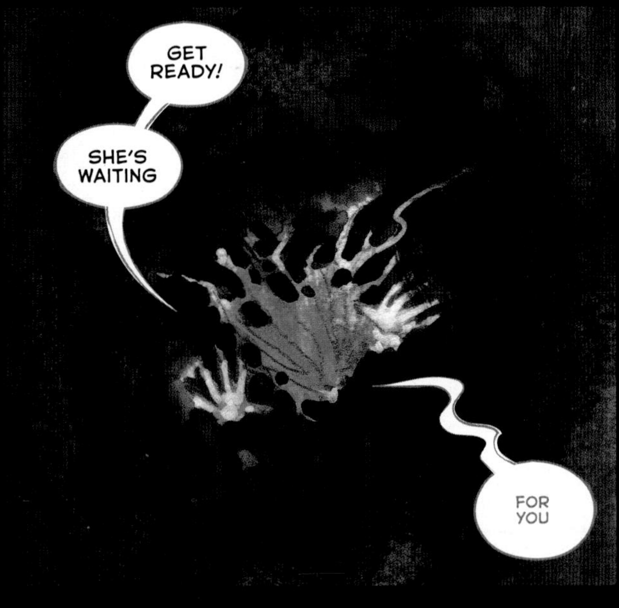
GET READY!
SHE'S WAITING
FOR YOU

UNDERWINTER

THE QUEEN OF SPIRITS

PART ONE

Philadelphia, Pennsylvania.

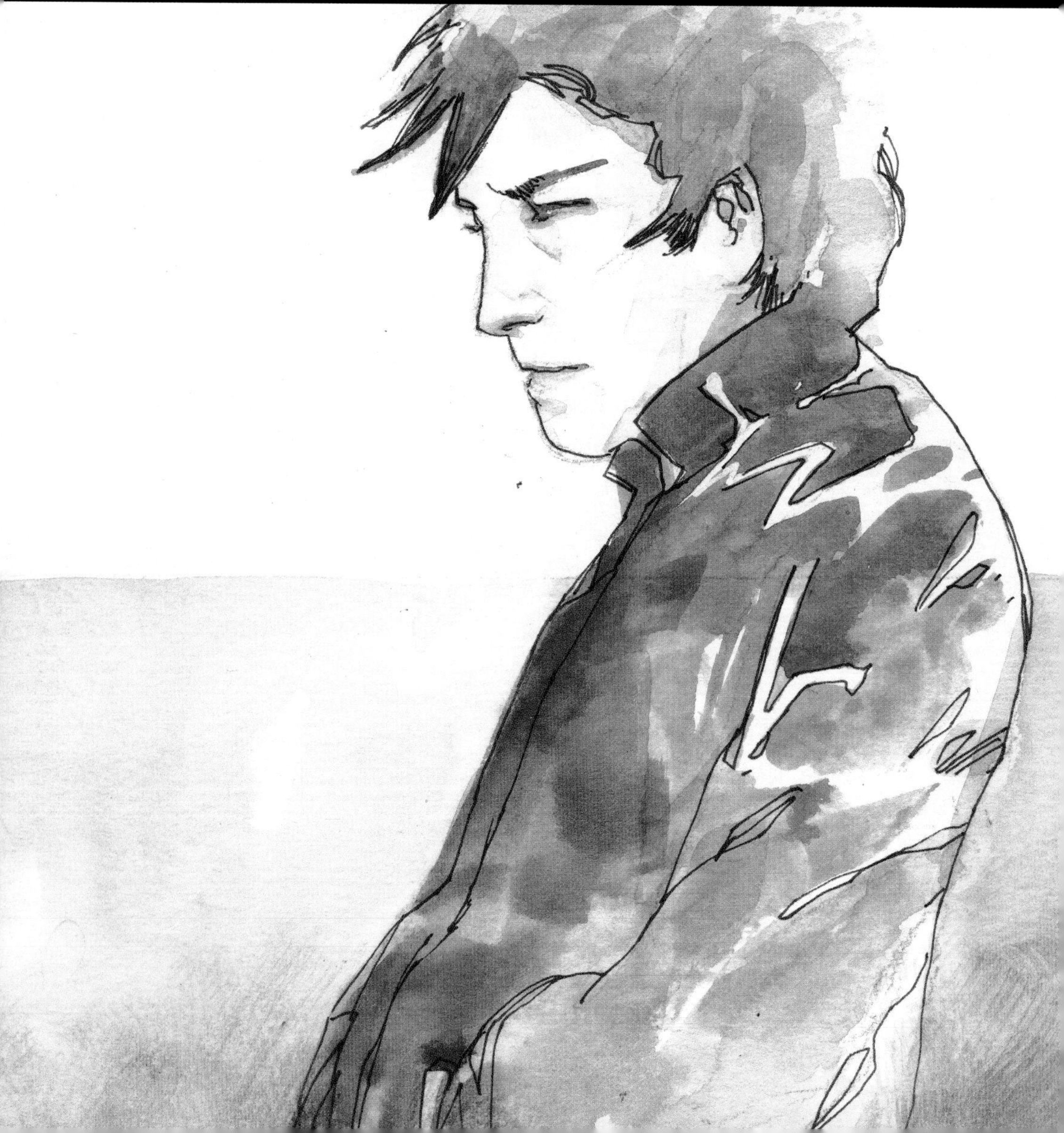

The trees are bare already, creaking forlornly, stripped of their whispering color.
Lipstick red leaves kissed away by autumn's cold wind.
Light seems to come from everywhere and nowhere.
They cast no shadows, the half-dead, undressed things. They barely seem to exist at all.
But they still surround us.
And they still reach towards the sun.

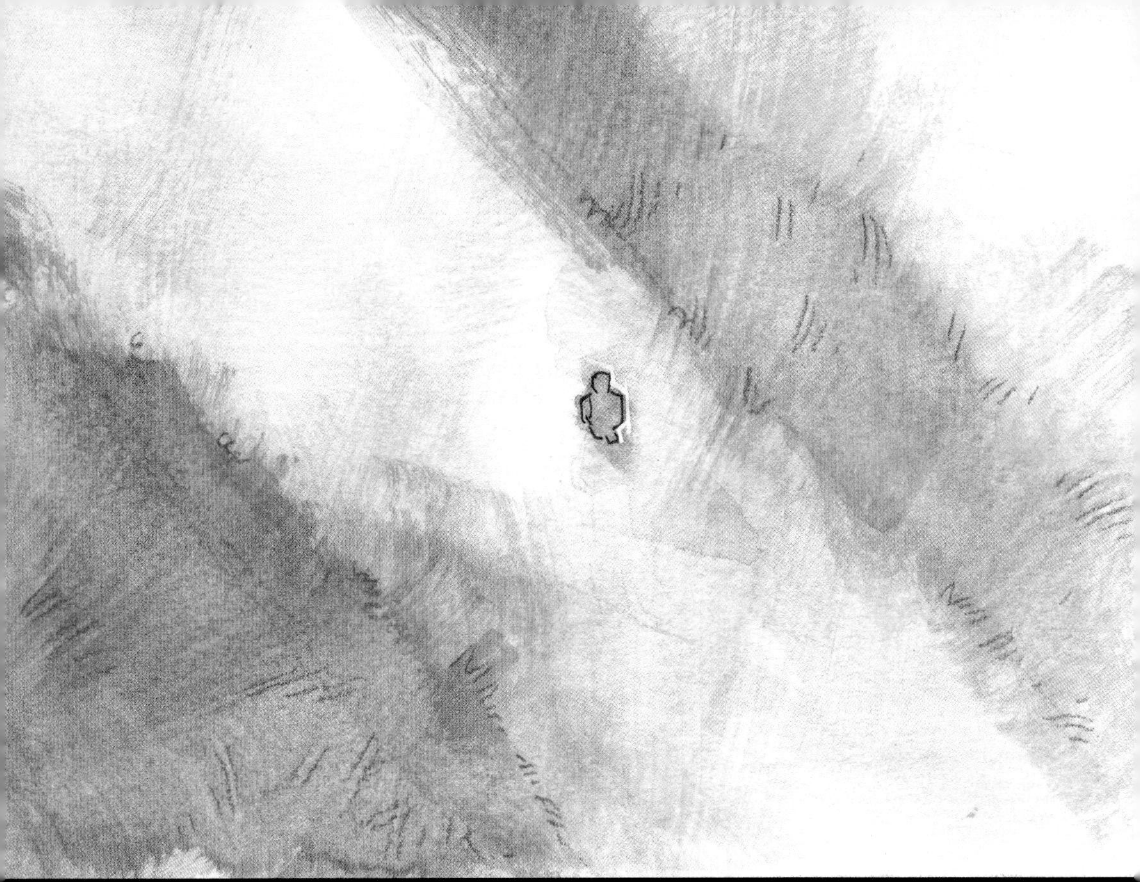

NOT THIS AGAIN.
SHE EDGES IN FORCE
SHH. THIS POOR GUY.
MISTER WILLIAMS?
DO YOU REMEMBER ME? ARE YOU FEELING OKAY?
HE'S NUTS. HE REELS OFF THIS NONSENSE ALL DAY. HE'S NOT HURT.
WE GOT BETTER THINGS TO DO, HUH?
I DO AT LEAST.
TOUCH THE GASPING DEAD MISTER
WHAT BEING BEHIND LEFT TO NOW
NO DEATH NO LITTLE FAMILIAR AIR
MISTER WILLIAMS.
THEY PUT YOU OUT ON THE STREET AGAIN, HUH?
HAMMER JESSICA HAMMER

WHAT BEING BEHIND LEFT TO NOW
INTERNAL BLUDGEONED BLEEDING FRACTURE MURDER MURDER
HAVE YOU EATEN? MISTER WILLIAMS?
HAVE YOU EATEN?
LEAVE HIM, ELLIS.
HE PUTS ALL THAT BLACK SHIT IN HIS NOSE AND MOUTH, I DON'T KNOW. HE EATS PAINT...INK.
EVERY TIME WE CHECK HIM OUT HE'S FINE. HE'S HEALTHIER THAN ME.
OH I HAVE EATEN MISTER WILLIAMS
CRYING NOT CRYING
HE NEEDS HELP, ORTIZ.
SURE, AND WE TAKE HIM IN, THEY WIPE HIS NOSE, THEY TURN HIM OUT AGAIN. A TO B TO C.
LET'S GO. GET SOME FUCKING LUNCH, SOMETHING. SPEAKING OF EATING.
YOU COMING?

LOOK, I KNOW YOU GOT THIS THING, YOU KNOW?
YOU NEED TO CARE FOR THE POOR DOWNTRODDEN AND ALL THE BEASTS OF THE FIELD, WHATEVER. YOU'RE A BELIEVER.
THAT'S FINE. THAT'S COOL.
SHIT LIKE WILLIAMS, PERSONALLY, IT GRINDS MY GEARS. HE'S DISGUSTING.
KSSSHK
WASTE OF TIME, OF RESOURCES. HE DOESN'T TAKE CARE OF HIMSELF.
I'M JUST HERE TO KEEP PEOPLE FROM DYING, IF I CAN. ACTUAL PEOPLE. CONTRIBUTING MEMBERS OF WHATEVER.
IF I CAN.
YOU KNOW?
SURE.
KSSSH EMS 3, ENGINE 2 RESPOND--
1700 RACE STREET FOR A STRUCK PEDESTRIAN, POSSIBLE HEAD INJURY, MAN IS UNRESPONSIVE.
LET'S GO.
1700 RACE STREET, DISPATCH.
WE'RE ON OUR WAY.
EEEOOEE

Blood red roses, held close to the chest. Blood red leaves scattered on asphalt, drying and curling.
The lights of an ambulance stain and then bleach the street, first one, then the other again.
IN THE SHADOW LIKE SMOKE
SHE BECKONS
THERE IS NO SHADOW
LIKE SMOKE THEY RISE

Two days after she was shot in the back of the head, Emma Pham has the funny feeling somebody is looking at her.
She turns around.
LIKE SMOKE THEY RISE.
HEY.
HEY!
DON'T I KNOW YOU FROM SOMEWHERE?

OH MY GOD, THAT SOUNDS LIKE A LINE. *HAHA.*
I'M JUST-- HOW LONG HAVE YOU BEEN WALKING?
I...I THINK I'M LOST. A WHILE. A FEW HOURS.
I'M NOT FROM AROUND HERE.
YOU'RE NOT?
YOU LOOK REALLY FAMILIAR.
WELL, YOU'RE NOT LOST, OKAY? YOU'RE--
COME WITH ME.
NO, I REALLY THINK I SHOULDN'T. I'VE BEEN WALKING--
YOU'VE BEEN WALKING AND YOU DON'T EVEN KNOW WHERE YOU'RE GOING.
I KNOW WHERE YOU'RE GOING.
MY NAME'S EMMA. I'M HEADED YOUR WAY.
WE ALL ARE.

WHAT-- WHAT DO YOU MEAN?
DAMN, I WISH I'D HAD THAT PIZZA I WAS THINKING ABOUT THE OTHER DAY.
I REMEMBER THINKING I SHOULDN'T BECAUSE I'D JUST BEEN TALKING ABOUT EATING HEALTHY.
WHAT DO YOU MEAN YOU KNOW WHERE I'M GOING?
LOOK.
GUNSHOT. MURDER MURDER.
WHO'S THIS?
I DON'T-- I DON'T WANT TO--
STERNUM FRACTURE.

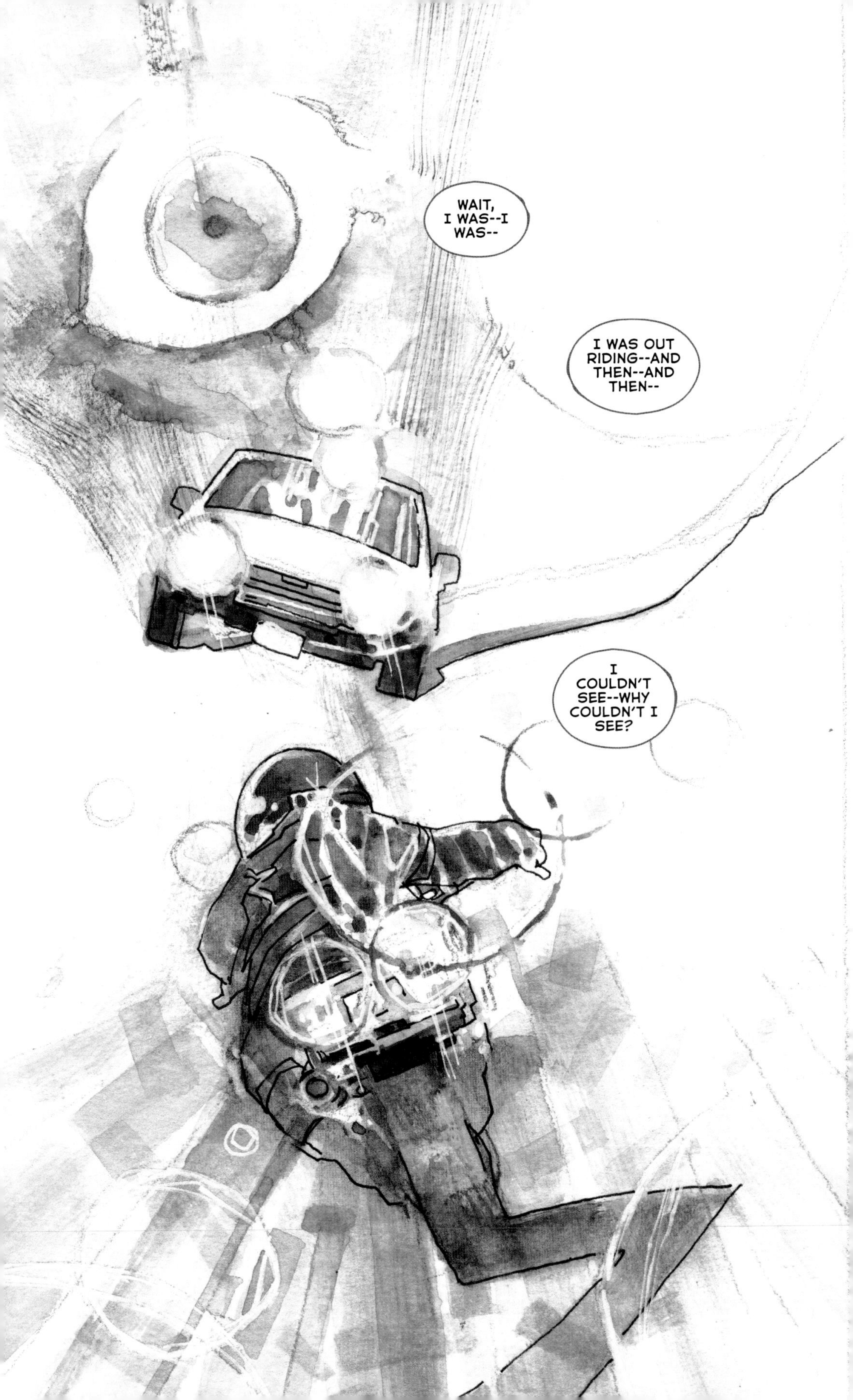
WAIT, I WAS--I WAS--
I WAS OUT RIDING--AND THEN--AND THEN--
I COULDN'T SEE--WHY COULDN'T I SEE?

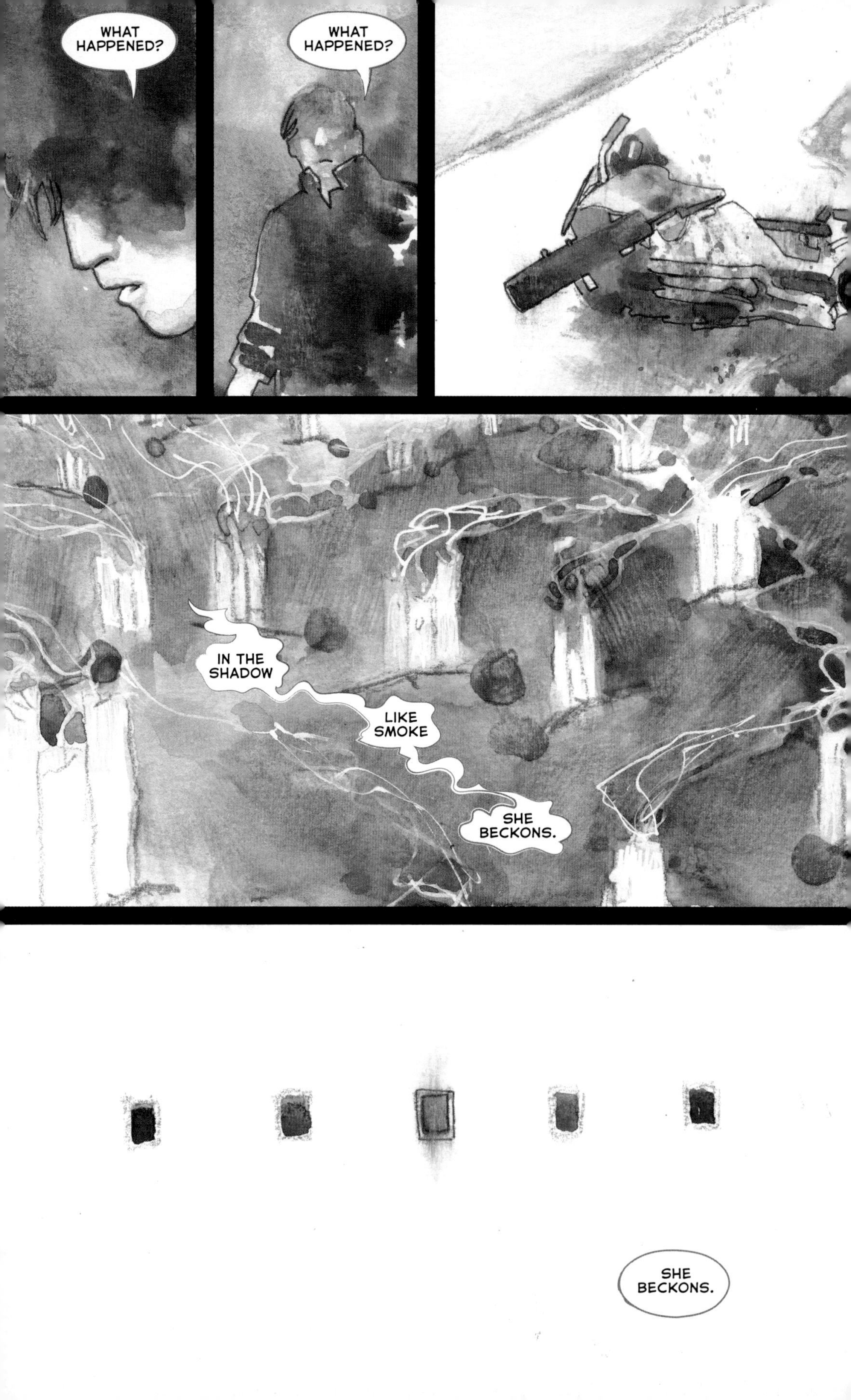
WHAT HAPPENED?
WHAT HAPPENED?
IN THE SHADOW
LIKE SMOKE
SHE BECKONS.
SHE BECKONS.

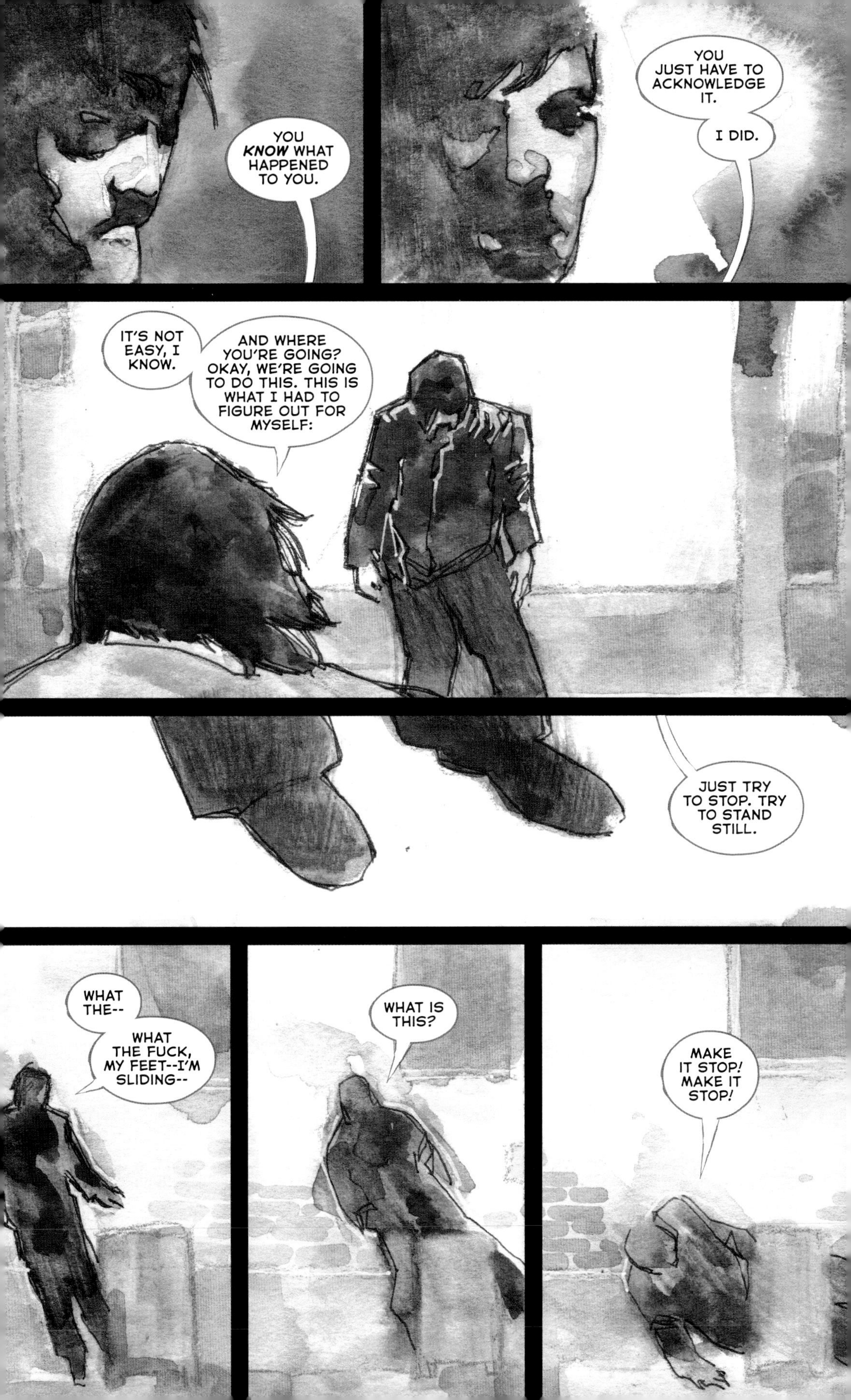
YOU KNOW WHAT HAPPENED TO YOU.
YOU JUST HAVE TO ACKNOWLEDGE IT.
I DID.
IT'S NOT EASY, I KNOW.
AND WHERE YOU'RE GOING? OKAY, WE'RE GOING TO DO THIS. THIS IS WHAT I HAD TO FIGURE OUT FOR MYSELF:
JUST TRY TO STOP. TRY TO STAND STILL.
WHAT THE--
WHAT THE FUCK, MY FEET--I'M SLIDING--
WHAT IS THIS?
MAKE IT STOP! MAKE IT STOP!

YOU CAN'T STOP. DON'T FREAK OUT.
JESUS. JESUS CHRIST!
THE SAME THING HAPPENS TO ME. TO ALL OF US. AND IF YOU LET IT HAPPEN YOU GO FASTER AND FASTER.
AAAA! HELP! HELP ME!
THE ONLY THING YOU CAN DO IS GET UP AND GO WITH IT. YOU HAVE TO WALK. THAT SLOWS IT DOWN.
GET UP AND WALK. STAND UP!
I'M COMING! I'LL CATCH UP.

1700 RACE. THAT'S JUST DOWN THE STREET FROM THE CITY COMPTROLLER'S OFFICE, Y'KNOW, IN THAT BUILDING WITH ALL THE RADIO STATIONS.
DISC JOCKEY SHITHEADS WITH THEIR EASY JOBS AND COFFEE SHOPS AND DAYCARE RIGHT IN THE BUILDING. ALL IN ONE PLACE BECAUSE ONE BULLSHIT COMPANY OWNS EVERYTHING NOW.
MY EX-WIFE'S BOYFRIEND WORKS THERE. ACCOUNTANT. PIECE OF SHIT.
BICYCLE DOWN, BET IT'S SOME SON OF A BITCH WHO WORKS THERE, THINKS HE OWNS THE ROAD. NO HELMET. RINGING HIS LITTLE BIKE BELL LIKE A PISSY PIECE OF--
GOD, YOU'RE AN ASSHOLE SOMETIMES.

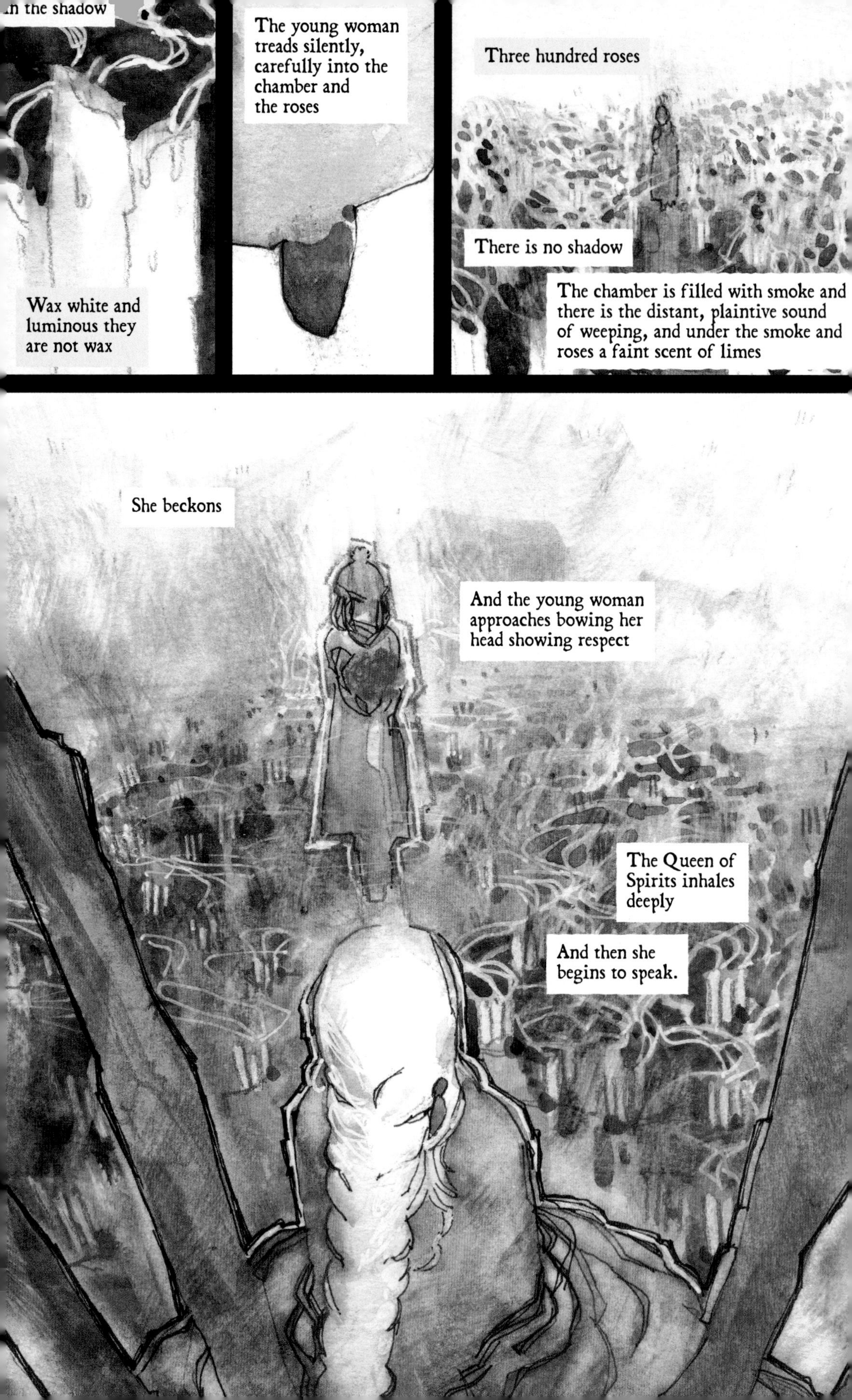
In the shadow
Wax white and luminous they are not wax
The young woman treads silently, carefully into the chamber and the roses
Three hundred roses
There is no shadow
The chamber is filled with smoke and there is the distant, plaintive sound of weeping, and under the smoke and roses a faint scent of limes
She beckons
And the young woman approaches bowing her head showing respect
The Queen of Spirits inhales deeply
And then she begins to speak.

UNDERWINTER

THE QUEEN OF SPIRITS

PART TWO

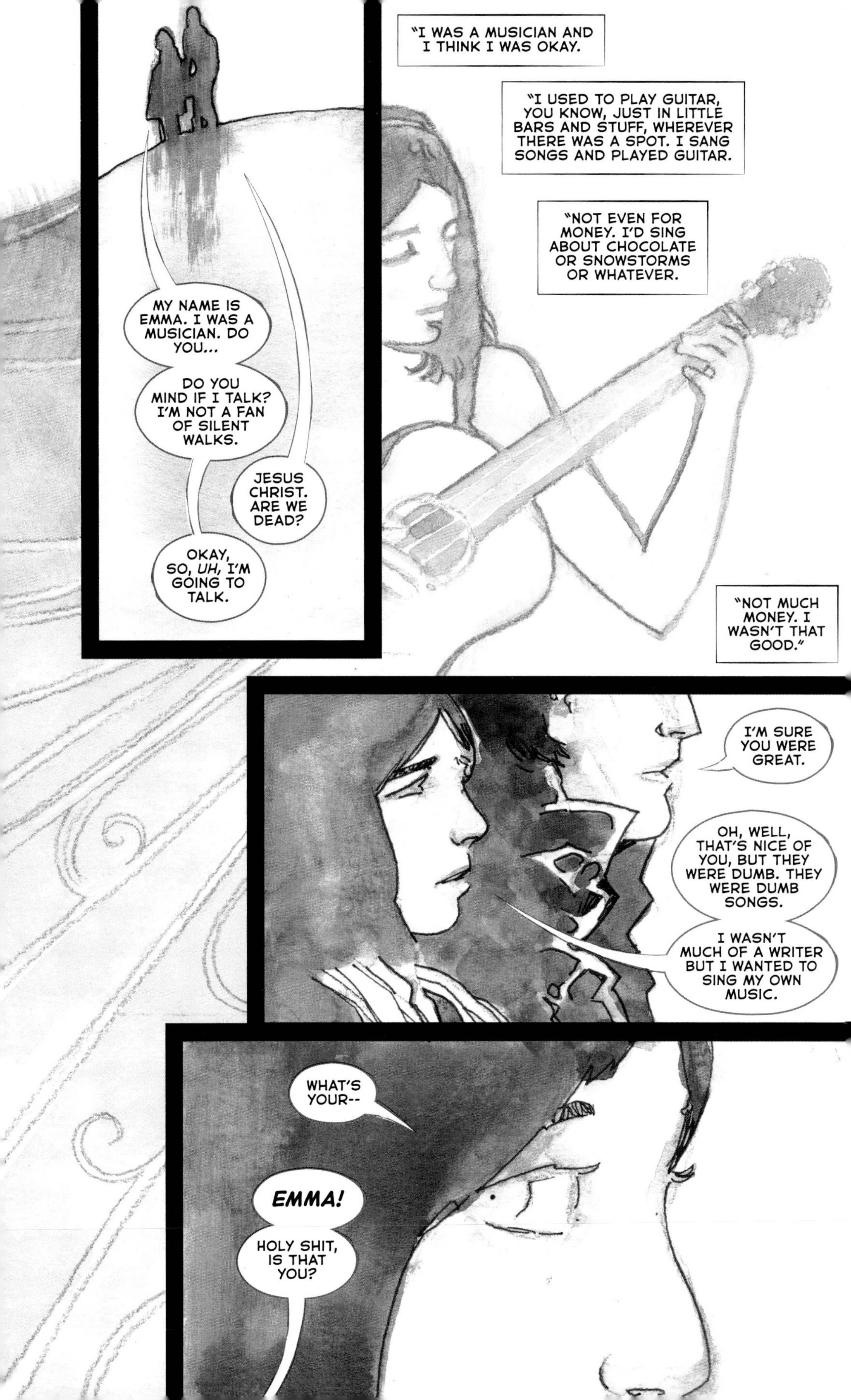

"I WAS A MUSICIAN AND I THINK I WAS OKAY.
MY NAME IS EMMA. I WAS A MUSICIAN. DO YOU...
DO YOU MIND IF I TALK? I'M NOT A FAN OF SILENT WALKS.
JESUS CHRIST. ARE WE DEAD?
OKAY, SO, *UH*, I'M GOING TO TALK.
"I USED TO PLAY GUITAR, YOU KNOW, JUST IN LITTLE BARS AND STUFF, WHEREVER THERE WAS A SPOT. I SANG SONGS AND PLAYED GUITAR.
"NOT EVEN FOR MONEY. I'D SING ABOUT CHOCOLATE OR SNOWSTORMS OR WHATEVER.
"NOT MUCH MONEY. I WASN'T THAT GOOD."
I'M SURE YOU WERE GREAT.
OH, WELL, THAT'S NICE OF YOU, BUT THEY WERE DUMB. THEY WERE DUMB SONGS.
I WASN'T MUCH OF A WRITER BUT I WANTED TO SING MY OWN MUSIC.
WHAT'S YOUR--
EMMA!
HOLY SHIT, IS THAT YOU?

IT IS YOU!
SHIT! HEY, REMEMBER ME?
WAKER?
OH MY GOD! OF COURSE I REMEMBER YOU!
WHAT ARE YOU DOING HERE?
AH SHIT, I WAS JUST ABOUT TO ASK YOU THAT.
BUT I GUESS WE'RE BOTH DOING THE SAME THING. DAMN. WHAT HAPPENED TO YOU?
NO WAIT, I DON'T WANNA KNOW. FUCK. I WANTED YOU TO BE SAFE. I ALWAYS WANTED YOU TO BE OKAY. SHIT. IT'S NOT FAIR.
HEY.
WHO'S THIS GUY?

OH LOOK.
NO HELMET.
AIRWAY'S PATENT, BREATHING GOOD.
PULSE IS FINE.
HE TOOK A TUMBLE. WITNESS SAID HE TOOK THE DOOR PRIZE, PASSENGER IN A PARKED CAR DIDN'T LOOK TO SEE HIM COMING UP.
NO BLOOD HERE.
GET THAT CERVICAL COLLAR ON.
YEAH. I DON'T SEE ANY BROKEN BONES.
PUPILS ARE FINE.
WHAT DO YOU THINK? LOAD N' GO?
I'LL CALL IT IN.

OKAY.
PROBABLY GOING TO WAKE UP AND TRY TO SUE OUR ASSES BECAUSE HE'S LATE FOR WORK.
WHEN HAS THAT EVER HAPPENED?
NEVER.
IT'S A PRETTY NICE DAY TODAY.
DON'T YOU THINK?
SURE. THERE'S A BICYCLE HERE IF YOU WANT TO TAKE A NICE RIDE AROUND THE--
BOOOOOOM!

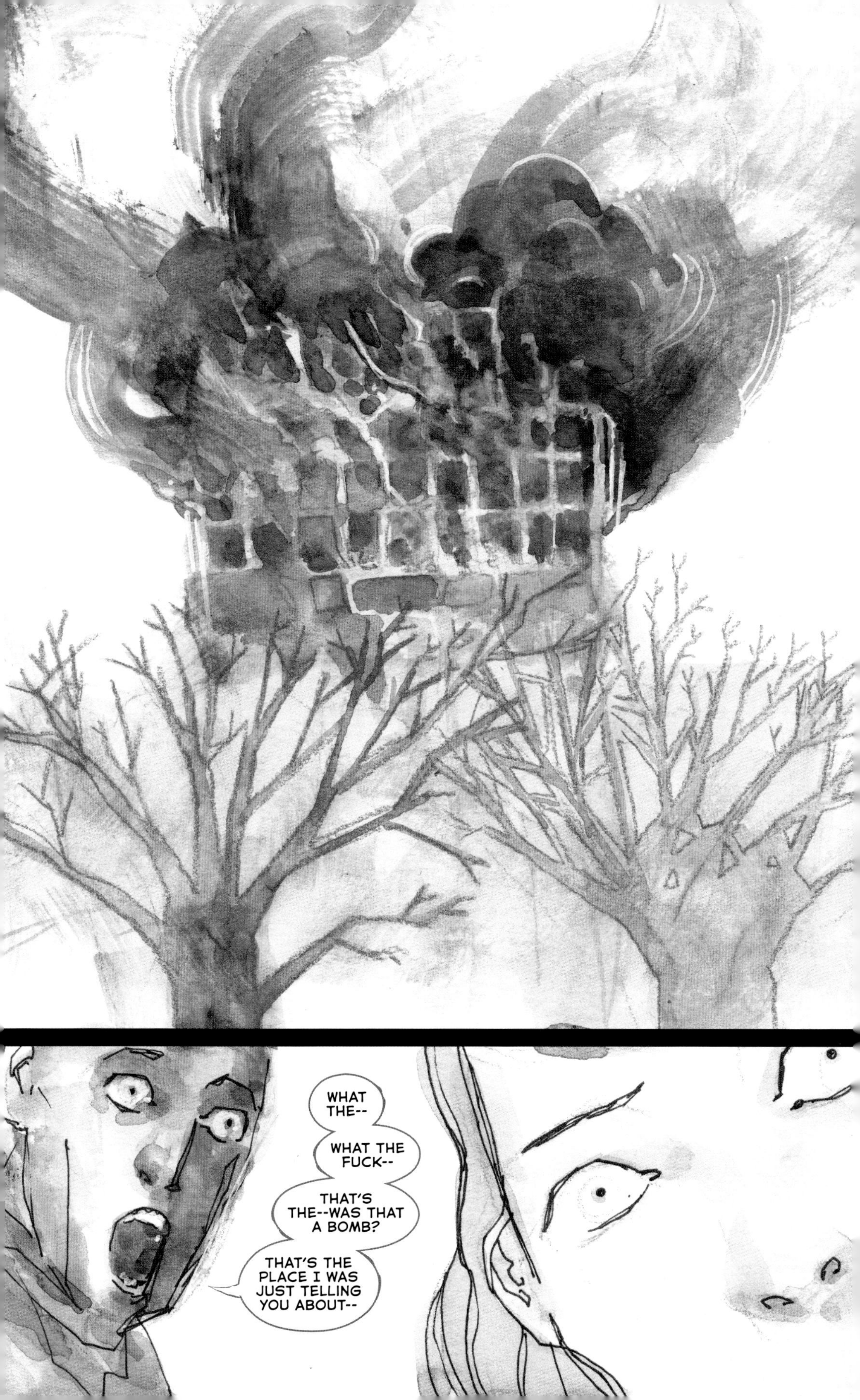
WHAT THE--
WHAT THE FUCK--
THAT'S THE--WAS THAT A BOMB?
THAT'S THE PLACE I WAS JUST TELLING YOU ABOUT--

HE LOOKS FAMILIAR.
HEY! WHAT'S YOUR NAME?
THAT'S WHAT I SAID!
I JUST MET HIM. HE'S PRETTY CONFUSED. I THINK HE WAS IN SOME KIND OF ACCIDENT.
HEY, WALK WITH US. WE WERE JUST TALKING.
MY NAME IS
CHRIS.
WE'RE ALL DEAD. YOU, ME, HER.
WE'RE ALL FUCKING DEAD. TALKING LIKE WE'RE AT A DINNER PARTY, ABOUT WHAT WE DO FOR A FUCKING LIVING.
WHY IS THIS OKAY? WHY AREN'T WE FREAKING OUT?

She reaches out
The windows sound a chime
The young woman listens and breathes softly across the candle wick
Just as she was taught
softly and cycling her breath
the glass chime grows
There is no flame
But the wick begins to smoke
It is not smoke
In shadow like smoke it rises

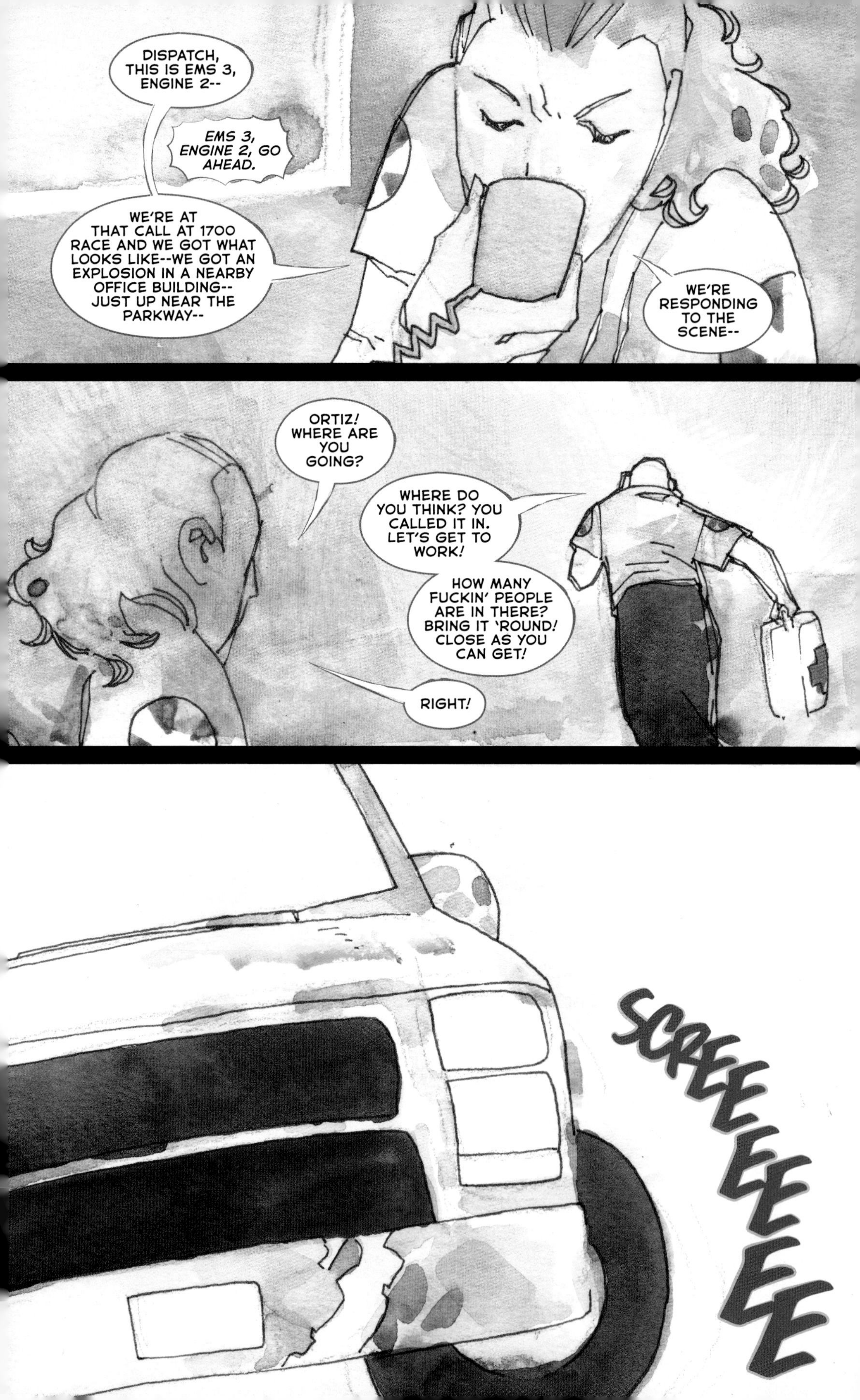

DISPATCH, THIS IS EMS 3, ENGINE 2--
EMS 3, ENGINE 2, GO AHEAD.
WE'RE AT THAT CALL AT 1700 RACE AND WE GOT WHAT LOOKS LIKE--WE GOT AN EXPLOSION IN A NEARBY OFFICE BUILDING-- JUST UP NEAR THE PARKWAY--
WE'RE RESPONDING TO THE SCENE--
ORTIZ! WHERE ARE YOU GOING?
WHERE DO YOU THINK? YOU CALLED IT IN. LET'S GET TO WORK!
HOW MANY FUCKIN' PEOPLE ARE IN THERE? BRING IT 'ROUND! CLOSE AS YOU CAN GET!
RIGHT!
SCREEEEEEEE

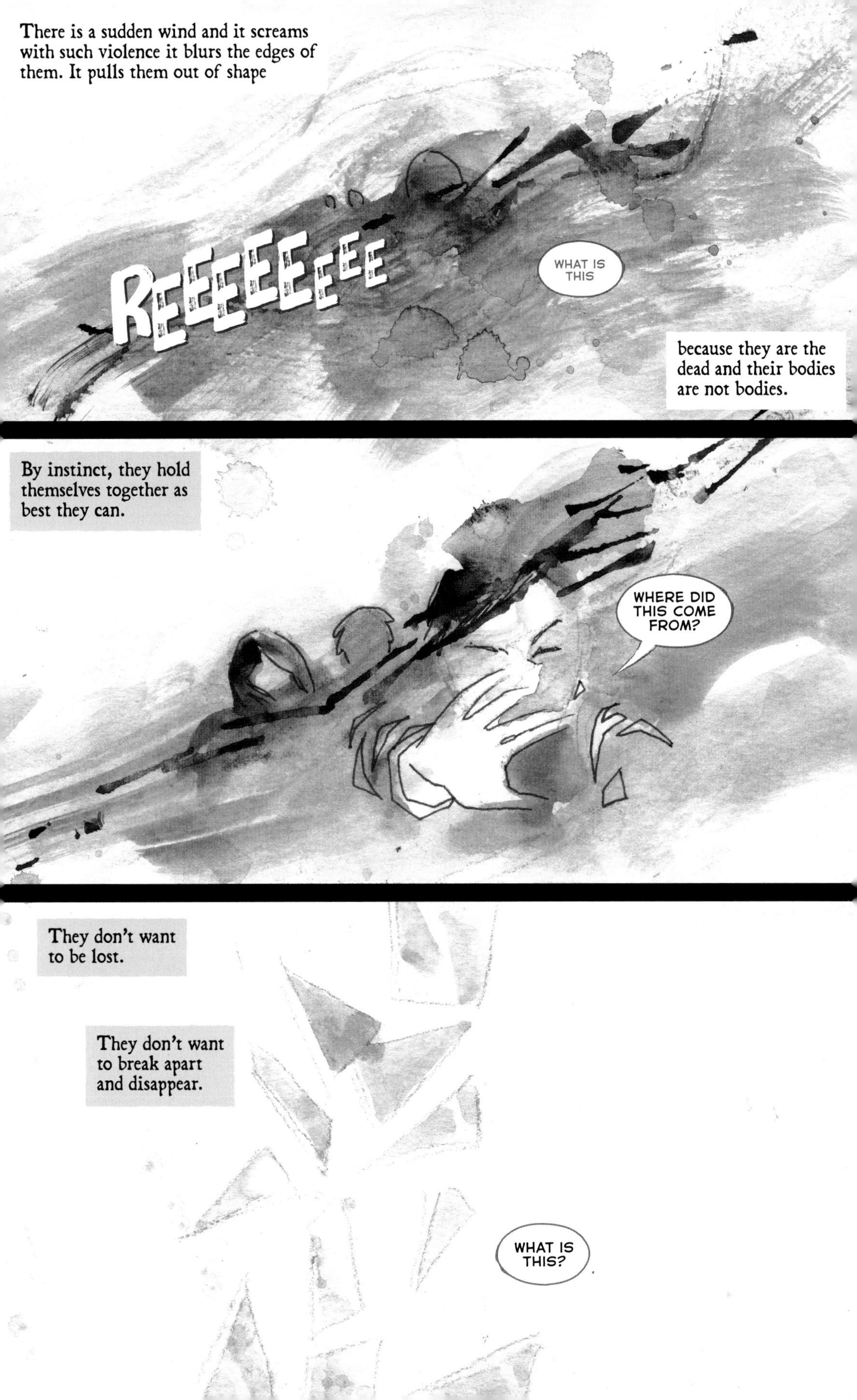
There is a sudden wind and it screams with such violence it blurs the edges of them. It pulls them out of shape
REEEEEEEE
WHAT IS THIS
because they are the dead and their bodies are not bodies.
By instinct, they hold themselves together as best they can.
WHERE DID THIS COME FROM?
They don't want to be lost.
They don't want to break apart and disappear.
WHAT IS THIS?

IT JUST--
OUT OF NOWHERE--
IT--
WHAT'S HAPPENING-- *HOLD ON! HOLD ON!*
Behind the screaming there is a chime
Is that the sound they hear now?

When the scream becomes a howl.
And the howl becomes a sigh.
And they open their eyes.
And they can see a building aflame
And at its base three hundred shapes rise
The chime sounds again. Three hundred shapes.
She beckons.

HOLY SHIT. HOLY SHIT.
WHAT WAS THAT? WAS THAT SOME KIND OF STORM?
I'M STILL HERE. HEY.
The chime fades.
ARE YOU STILL HERE?
Y-YEAH.
I THINK THERE'S SOME-THING--CHRIST. AH, CHRIST.
I DON'T WANT IT TO BE WHAT I THINK IT IS.
BACK THERE. DO YOU SEE THEM?
PEOPLE. LIKE US.
A WHOLE FUCKING LOT OF PEOPLE.
I SEE THEM. ALL TOGETHER. IS THAT WHAT THEY ARE?
WHERE ARE THEY ALL COMING FROM?

THEY'RE GOING TO SEE HER.
JESUS. JESUS CHRIST.
THAT'S A LOT OF--WHAT KILLED THEM ALL? ALL AT ONCE LIKE THAT...
...IMAGINE WHAT IT'S LIKE IN THAT CROWD.
WON'T HAVE TO IMAGINE FOR LONG. YOU CAN ASK THEM SOON. MAYBE.
THEY'RE HEADED WHERE WE ARE. DAMN, MAN, LOOK AT THEM COMING ON LIKE A WAVE.
TO SEE THE QUEEN OF SPIRITS. JUST LIKE US. TO MAKE THEIR CASE SO SHE CAN DECIDE WHO IS SPARED...
...AND WHO GOES INTO THE DARK.

GRRAH!
I GOT-- THERE'S SOMEONE HERE!

AH FUCK.
THIS ONE'S GONE. POOR GUY.
SHIT. FUCK!
EVERYBODY JUST CAME IN TO GO TO WORK. JUST AN ORDINARY DAY.
OKAY. OKAY. YOU TRAINED FOR THIS. YOU'RE READY FOR THIS. THINK. LISTEN. THERE ARE SURVIVORS. THERE HAVE TO BE SURVIVORS.
HEY! HEY YOU IN THERE!
GET OUT OF THERE!
IT'S NOT SAFE IN THERE!
IS--DID YOU FIND ANYBODY ALIVE IN THERE?

ORTIZ!
I'M IN HERE. THIS WAY.
LISTEN. CAN YOU HEAR THEM?
CRYING AND COUGHING. HOW MANY PEOPLE TRAPPED IN THIS PLACE, YOU THINK?
WE GOTTA PULL 'EM OUT, ELLIS.
HOLD UP!
PULL BACK! PARTS OF THIS PLACE ARE STILL COLLAPSING!
DON'T LISTEN TO THAT FUCKIN' PRICK.
FUCKIN' COWARD.
THERE WAS A DAYCARE IN THIS PLACE. I HEARD SOMETHING THAT WAY. LIKE A... SOMEONE CRYING. COME ON.
WE'RE EMS!
SEARCH AND RESCUE!
...WON'T HELP ANYONE IF YOU GET TRAPPED TOO, YOU IDIOTS...
THANKS FOR THE WARNING, USELESS PIECE OF SHIT. COME ON...

ELLIS!
OVER HERE!
JESUS. JESUS. THREE, MAYBE FOUR YEARS OLD...
LET ME CLEAR THIS AWAY. OH DAMN, DAMN--
IS SHE BREATHING?
BRINGING ONE DOWN
THERE'S MORE. THERE'S MORE IN HERE.
PLEASE GOD.
NNNH
PLEASE...

I GOT-- I CAN'T FIND A PULSE.
SHE'S BREATHING BUT I CAN'T FIND A FUCKING PULSE. YOU WANT TO WAIT UNTIL THIS PLACE IS STABLE? FUCKING ASSHOLES!
EASY. WE'LL TAKE HER, BUDDY.
LET'S GET HER CLEAR AND HAVE A LOOK.
DID YOU SEE MORE IN THERE? ARE THERE MORE?
DID I-- LOOK AT THE SIZE OF THIS PLACE!
WHAT DO YOU THINK?
TAKE HER. I'M GOING BACK IN.
HEY. VISIBILITY IS FOR SHIT IN THERE. ALL THIS DUST AND SMOKE KICKING UP.
HANG BACK A MINUTE, ALL RIGHT? SEE THE LIGHTS? EVERYONE IS ON THEIR WAY. EMERGENCY RESPONSE. THEY'RE COMING TO HELP.
YEAH? TELL THEM HELLO FROM ME AND FUCK YOU FOR WAITING.
I'M GOING IN.

UNDERWINTER

THE QUEEN OF SPIRITS

PART THREE

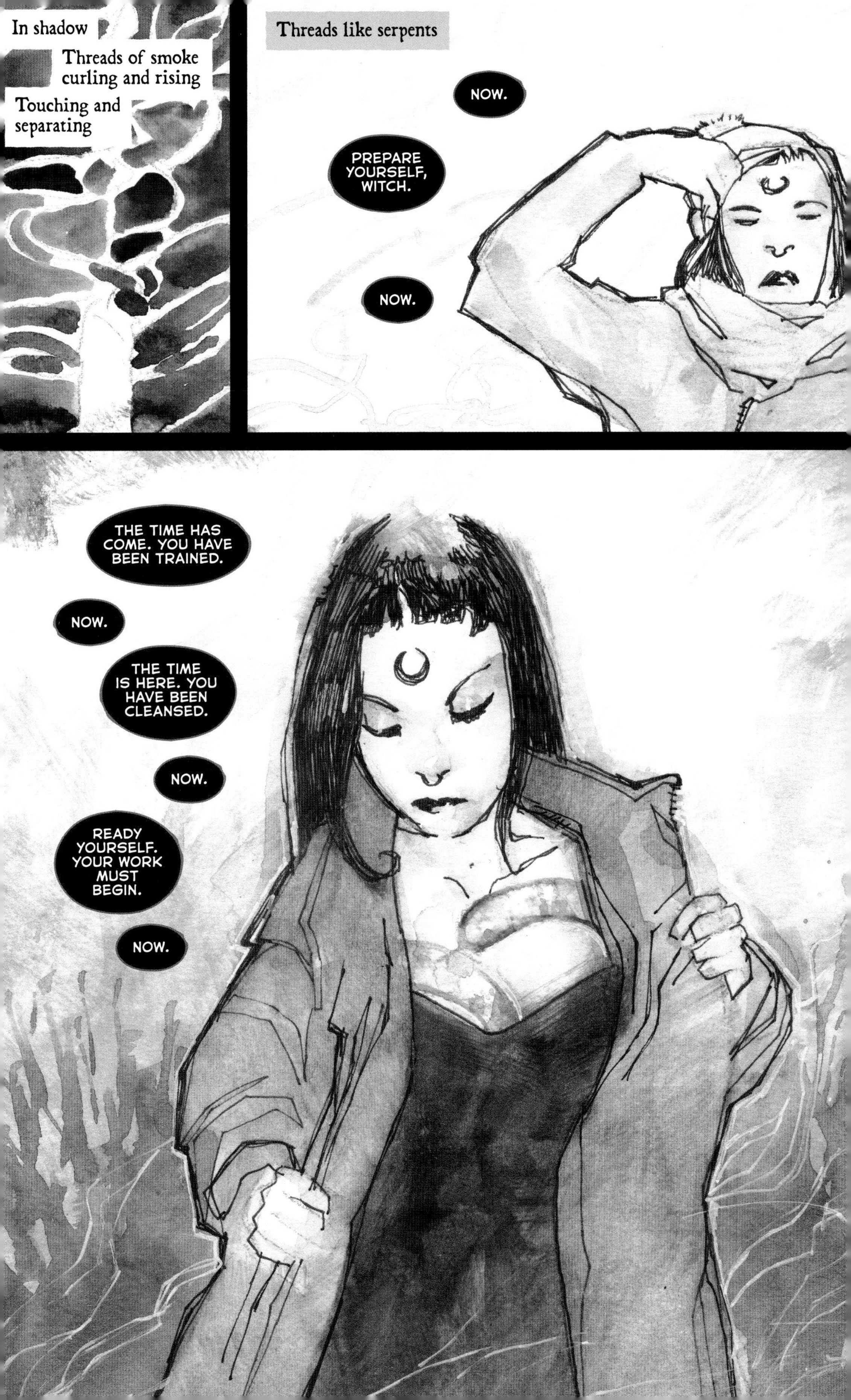

In shadow
Threads of smoke curling and rising
Touching and separating
Threads like serpents
NOW.
PREPARE YOURSELF, WITCH.
NOW.
THE TIME HAS COME. YOU HAVE BEEN TRAINED.
NOW.
THE TIME IS HERE. YOU HAVE BEEN CLEANSED.
NOW.
READY YOURSELF. YOUR WORK MUST BEGIN.
NOW.

AW HELL.

A serpent threads in shadow, curling as cloth drops whispering to the floor
Ten thousand candles ten thousand roses
There are no flames
Smoke rises and curls in shadow like smoke
She inhales deeply and opens her eyes

I DON'T RECOGNIZE THIS PLACE. WHAT PART OF TOWN ARE WE IN?
IS THIS EVEN A REAL PLACE?
HEY, CHRIS. LET ME ASK YOU SOMETHING.
SHE'S A STEP AHEAD OF YOU, I'M TEN STEPS BEHIND.
HOW COME WE BOTH HEARD OF THE QUEEN OF SPIRITS AND YOU NEVER DID?
LOOK-- THERE'S SOMEONE UP AHEAD.
HEY!
YOU THERE!
CAN YOU SEE ANYTHING UP AHEAD?
ARE WE CLOSE? ARE WE CLOSE TO HER?
HE'S GONE.
WELL, HE'S MOVING. LIKE WE ALL ARE.
MAYBE HE'LL ANSWER.

MAYBE NOT.
WE'RE HERE NOW ANYWAY.
LET'S SEE WHAT WE CAN SEE.
WE SHOULD TELL THE ONES BEHIND US.
ABOUT THE QUEEN.
SO THEY CAN GET READY FOR HER.

GET WHAT READY?
THIS STORY ABOUT THIS QUEEN. YOU JUST BELIEVE IT?
IT SOUNDS LIKE SANTA CLAUS TO ME. IT SOUNDS LIKE THE TOOTH FAIRY. WHAT IF IT'S BULLSHIT? I HAVE TO, WHAT, I HAVE TO BE HONEST ABOUT MYSELF AND SHE'LL GIVE ME A PRIZE. IS THAT RIGHT?
WHY WOULDN'T IT BE TRUE?
I BELIEVE IT BECAUSE IT'S WHAT'S HAPPENING. THE OTHERS HAVE BEEN PASSING IT BACK--SHE'S UP AHEAD. THERE ARE PEOPLE WHO HAVE ALREADY SEEN HER.
YEAH?
WHERE ARE THEY? I MEAN IF THEY'RE FREE. IF SHE SHOWED THEM HER MERCY AND THEY'RE SET FREE. WHY HAVEN'T ANY OF THEM COME BACK TO TELL US IT'S ALL TRUE?
IT IS TRUE.
WE SHOULD TELL THEM.
YOU'RE NOT *LISTENING*

The sound the only sound
A hiss exhaled slowly as she twists in shadow
As she curls and uncurls in the way she was taught. In the way she practiced for years, as a child in the dusk, as a young woman, for years and years.
Her body moves without thought. She is like smoke. She is drawing the shape that is needed.
And it begins to hurt
And there is the scent of limes

She cycles her breath and the hiss does not stop.
And she weeps ink that is not ink.
Smoke threads from her fingertips, phantom trails that curl and connect and separate
The pain intensifies and she is blinded by black tears and she feels a sudden rising stab of perverse arousal and she wants to laugh or scream

CORONER
MORE COMING OUT. GET READY.
ANY OF THEM ALIVE?
LOTS MORE COMING OUT.
IN HERE, ELLIS.
YOU WITH ME?

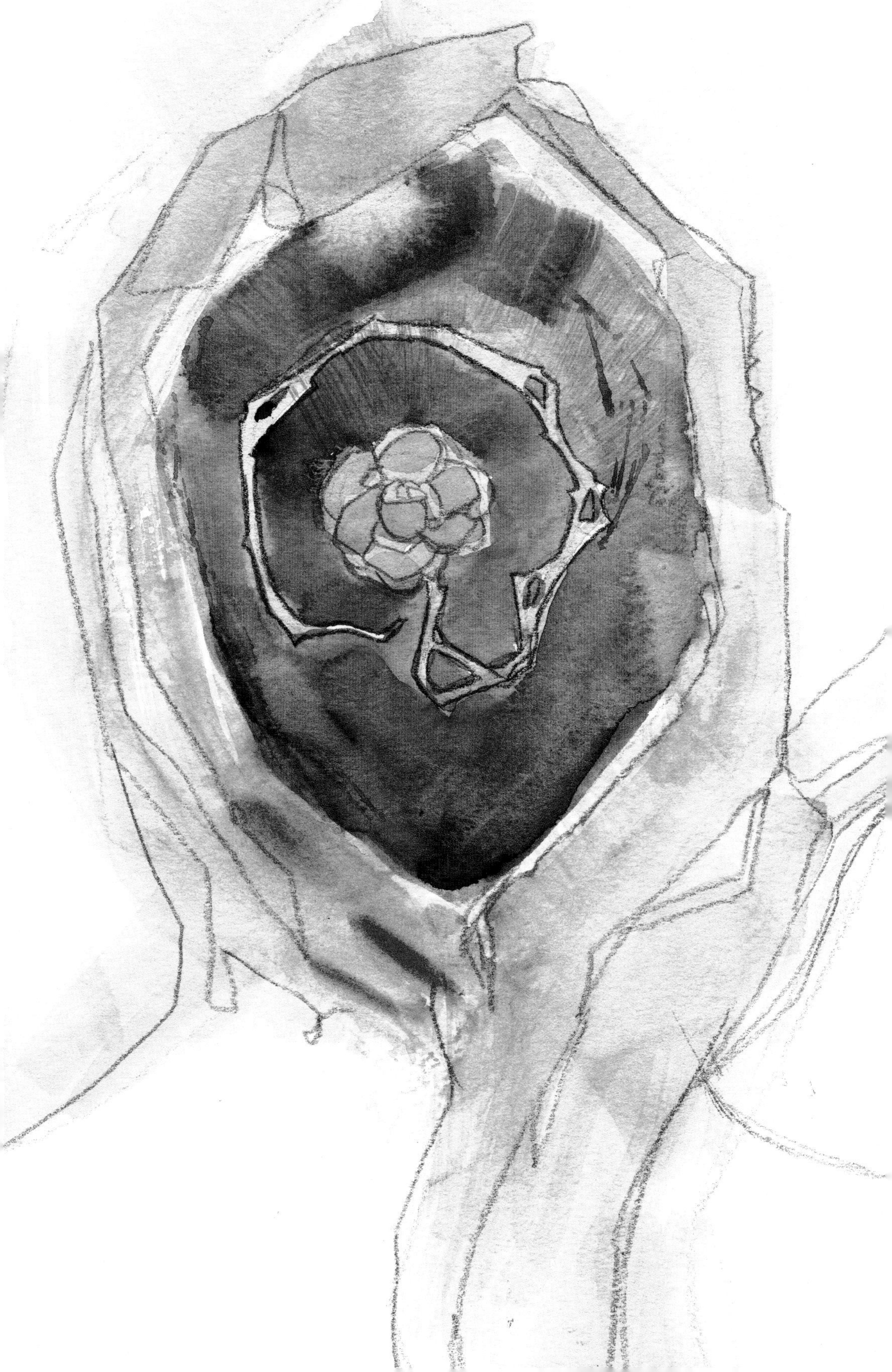

DAMN IT.
GODDAMN IT.
ORTIZ.
I'M WITH YOU.
YOU NEED A HAND?
THIS ONE'S GONE TOO. THEY'RE ALL FUCKING GONE.
THAT LITTLE GIRL, SHE DIDN'T MAKE IT, DID SHE?
YEAH I NEED A HAND. HELP ME PULL THESE PIPES OUT OF THIS POOR BASTARD SO I CAN GET HIM OUT OF THIS HELLHOLE.

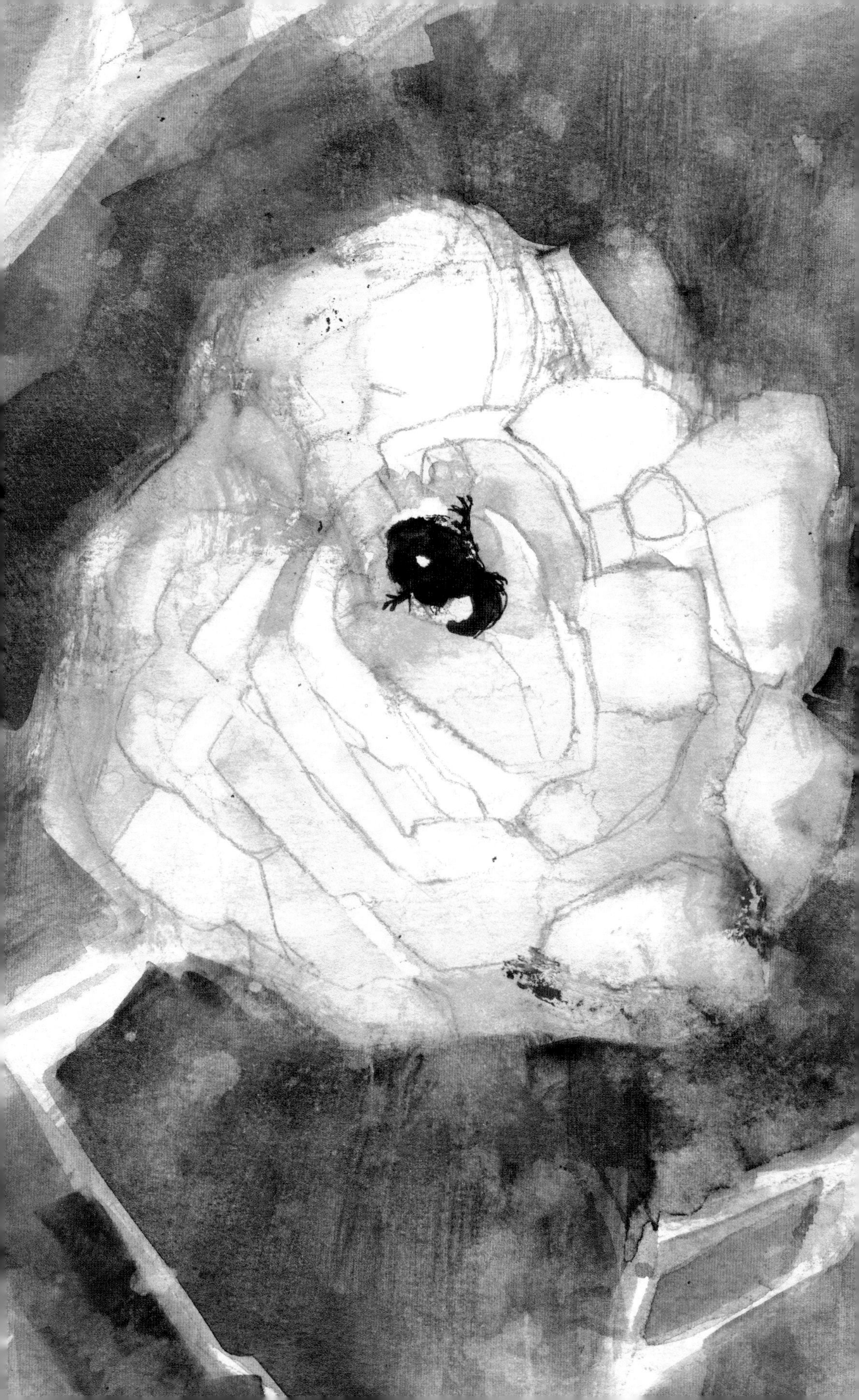

FRANKLIN IS OUT THERE. WITH THE FIRE MARSHAL. REMEMBER HIM?
HE SAYS IT WAS A BOMB.
SAYS IT WAS PROBABLY JUST ONE BUT THEY'RE SWEEPING TO SEE IF THERE ARE MORE.
"JUST ONE," BUT THE WHOLE PLACE CAME DOWN AND WE CAN'T FIND A SINGLE SURVIVOR. I TOLD HIM--I KNEW WHAT YOU'D SAY SO I SAID IT FOR BOTH OF US.
I TOLD HIM WE WERE GOING TO KEEP SEARCHING WHILE THEY DID THEIR SWEEP.
WE HAVE TO FIND SOMEONE. THERE HAS TO BE SOMEONE.
I TOLD HIM WE'RE AWARE OF THE RISKS.
FUCKIN' A.

The Queen of Spirits looks up from beneath her hooded cowl, her arthritic hands clasped tight, fingers dry like bone.
There is no turning back. Her eyelids rasp, her eyes burning. The girl is dancing. The one she raised like a daughter.
There has been no turning back for some years now.
And she is tired and old and she ran out of tears long, long ago.

TEN THOUSAND STRANDS.
TEN THOUSAND SONGS.
TEN THOUSAND BREATHS.
TEN THOUSAND CUTS.

ORTIZ!
I LOST YOU FOR A--
ORTIZ! WHERE'D YOU GO?
LIKE A MAZE IN HERE...
DON'T START TALKING TO YOURSELF, GIRL. DON'T START CRACKING UP. THERE'S WORK TO DO.
ORTIZ!

HERE
THERE'S ONE HERE.
OKAY. OKAY.
ELLIS! HOLY SHIT!
I FOUND A LIVE ONE!
COME QUICK!
I GOT ONE HERE, HE'S A LITTLE BANGED UP BUT HE'S GOOD. FUCKING HELL I TOLD YOU, I TOLD YOU WE'D FIND SURVIVORS!
THAT'S GREAT. JESUS THAT'S GREAT.
I'M COMING. LET'S GET HIM OUT OF HERE.

JUST HOLD--
RRRRUMMMMBBBLLEEE

UNDERWINTER

THE QUEEN OF SPIRITS

PART FOUR

THEY ARE HIDDEN.
THEY ARE AMONG US AND THEY ARE DRIVING US MAD.
THEY BLEED THEMSELVES INTO US.
AND WE ARE IN SUCH PAIN AND SUCH DESPAIR
AND BECAUSE WE DO NOT KNOW THE SOURCE, BECAUSE IT IS UNSEEN
WE LASH OUT
BLINDLY VIOLENT
WE ARE LOST
BUT WE WILL SEE WE ARE LOST BUT WE WILL

"REVEAL THE ENEMY."

I CAUGHT A GLIMPSE OF THEM WHEN I WAS YOUR AGE. WHEN I WAS YOUNG. JUST A GLIMPSE.
THEY HATE US SO MUCH. THEY WANT US SICK. THEY WANT US IN PAIN, INFLICTING IT ON OURSELVES AND EACH OTHER ENDLESSLY, ENDLESSLY.
THEY POISON US.
THEIR GREATEST STRENGTH IS THEIR INVISIBILITY. THEY MOVE AMONG US, WATCHING US FLAIL HELPLESSLY, HOPELESSLY.
HELP ME NOW. I RAISED YOU FOR THIS. I GAVE MY LIFE FOR THIS.

WE'RE HERE. CAN YOU FEEL IT?
WE'RE FINALLY HERE.

OH MY GOD.
I'M SO HAPPY. IT'S ALL TRUE! IT IS! I KNOW IT!
SHE'S IN THERE WAITING!

I'M JUST--LISTEN, SOMETHING'S PULLING US IN THERE.
IF SHE'S IN THERE AND SHE'S GOING TO HELP US, WHY WOULD WE HAVE TO BE PULLED IN WHETHER WE WANT TO GO OR NOT?
DON'T BE STUPID.
IT'S SO WE DON'T GET LOST.
YOU REMEMBER HOW CONFUSED YOU WERE.
I'M STILL CONFUSED.
YOU BELIEVE THIS STORY. I'M NOT SO SURE.
WHAT IF SHE'S NOT REAL?
WHAT IF THERE'S SOMETHING TERRIBLE IN THERE?
YOU'RE JUST AFRAID.
IT'S OKAY. YOU'LL BE FINE.
YOU JUST HAVE TO LET YOUR FEAR GO. YOU JUST HAVE TO OPEN UP AND BE HONEST ABOUT YOURSELF AND YOU'LL BE FORGIVEN. YOU'LL BE FINE.

"HONEST ABOUT MYSELF...
"I WAS RIDING FAST. REALLY FAST. I COULDN'T SEE--WHY COULDN'T I SEE?
"WHY COULDN'T I SEE..."
I REMEMBER. AH, HELL.
BE HONEST ABOUT MYSELF. I HAVE TO DO THIS OUT LOUD? LIKE CONFESSION? YOU'RE A GOOD PERSON, YOU PROBABLY DON'T HAVE MUCH TO SAY.
ME? AH, HELL.
I DON'T THINK I SHOULD SAY ANYTHING. I DON'T THINK THAT'S GOING TO HELP ANYBODY.

MNUH--
GGGHUH!
H-HEY. SHIT. IT ALL CAME DOWN. SHIT.
CAN YOU HEAR ME?
ORTIZ, ARE YOU THERE?
She beckons

CRACK
AAAA!
WHOK
CAN YOU HEAR ME?
I HEAR YOU
I'M HERE.
OH, THANK GOD.
THANK YOU, GOD.

YOU'RE A YOUNG, MODERN PROFESSIONAL...
I'M COMING. YOU'RE GOING TO BE OKAY.
DON'T TELL ME YOU'RE GONNA GET IRRATIONAL IN HERE.
FIND RELIGION.
WHAT? I'M HERE.
TAKE MY HAND. THE ROOF CAVED IN. WE'RE GOING TO GET YOU OUT OF HERE.
I HEARD YOU PRAYING.
She beckons

I AM IN HERE WITH YOU.
YOU ARE IN HERE WITH ME.
THE FINAL SACRIFICES ARE ON THEIR WAY. AFTER ALL THIS TIME. YOU'VE DONE SO WELL. YOU'RE ALMOST FINISHED.

ALL THIS TIME. IT WAS NEVER OUR FAULT. ALL THE TERRIBLE THINGS THAT HAPPENED IN THIS WORLD.
ALL THE BLOOD AND RAGE AND MADNESS AND DESPAIR.
WE WERE ONLY WEAK.
WE WERE ONLY PREY.
TEAR THEIR CAMOUFLAGE AWAY! CALL THEM FORTH FROM THE SHADOW!
WE WILL SEE THEM TOWERING OVER OUR HOMES.
SHOW THEM TO THE WORLD, THAT WE MAY TAKE UP ARMS AGAINST THEM! AGAINST *THEM!*

HEY. TOMMY.
IT'S TIME. IT'S HAPPENING TODAY. YOU GOT MY LIST?
I DON'T WANT TO KNOW.
YEAH, I GOT YOUR LIST. A HUNDRED MUSICIANS. LOCALS.
YOU GOT MY MONEY?
FIVE HUNDRED BUCKS, HERE YOU GO.
NOT BAD FOR JUST A LIST OF NAMES, *HUH?*
YOU WANT TO TAKE YOURSELF A VACATION? YOU EARNED IT. YOU GONNA GO FOR A RIDE? YOU LIKE TO TAKE A RIDE ON SUNDAYS, DON'T YOU?
FUCK DO YOU CARE?

REVEAL THE ENEMY.
REVEAL THE ENEMY.
REVEAL THE ENEMY.
REVEAL THE ENEMY.

"I COULDN'T SEE BECAUSE I WAS CRYING.
"CRYING INSIDE MY VISOR AND I DIDN'T FLIP IT UP, I JUST WENT FASTER AND FASTER.
"BECAUSE I FOUND OUT WHAT THEY DID.
"TO THE PEOPLE ON THAT LIST."
CHRIS? I'M AT THE WALL.
I CAN FEEL IT...LIKE I'M GETTING LIGHTER, LIKE I'M GOING TO FLY...
THIS IS IT. IT'S REALLY HAPPENING.
THIS IS YOUR CHANCE. APPROACH HER WITH HONESTY. YOU KNOW SHE'S REAL. TELL HER WHO YOU REALLY ARE AND SHE'LL SPARE YOU--
THAT'S WHAT THEY SAY!

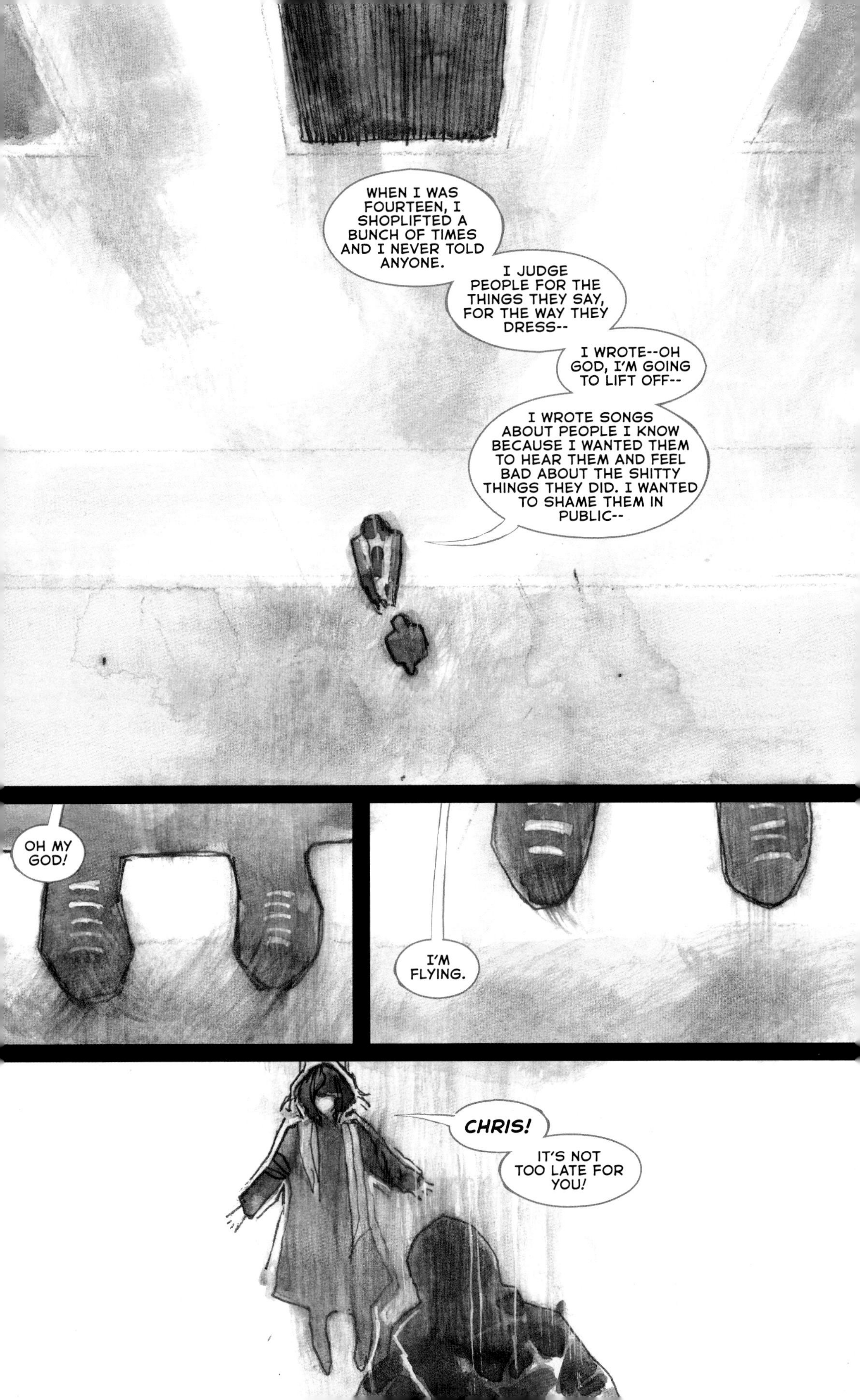
WHEN I WAS FOURTEEN, I SHOPLIFTED A BUNCH OF TIMES AND I NEVER TOLD ANYONE.
I JUDGE PEOPLE FOR THE THINGS THEY SAY, FOR THE WAY THEY DRESS--
I WROTE--OH GOD, I'M GOING TO LIFT OFF--
I WROTE SONGS ABOUT PEOPLE I KNOW BECAUSE I WANTED THEM TO HEAR THEM AND FEEL BAD ABOUT THE SHITTY THINGS THEY DID. I WANTED TO SHAME THEM IN PUBLIC--
OH MY GOD!
I'M FLYING.
CHRIS!
IT'S NOT TOO LATE FOR YOU!

YOU CAN DO IT!
NO.
NO, I REALLY CAN'T.
NOT IN FRONT OF EMMA, YOU CAN'T.
AM I RIGHT?
BECAUSE FIRST OF ALL, STOP ME IF I'M WRONG, YOU WEASELLY MOTHERFUCKER--
--YOUR NAME AIN'T CHRIS.

I'M A LIAR.
WHAT?
ARE YOU HURT? I'M GONNA DIG YOU OUT.
ELLIS. I KNOW YOU THINK I'M AN ASSHOLE.
YOU'RE RIGHT.
I FELL, THERE'S SOMETHING PUH--PUNCHED INTO MY BACK.
I'M GOING INTO SHOCK--I CAN ALREADY TELL I'M NOT GOING TO MAKE IT.
YOU'RE RIGHT ABOUT ME. LISTEN, I STOLE FROM THE DISPENSARY, I DID--I DID THINGS--I THOUGHT I COULD MAYBE BALANCE THE SCALES, THE BAD THINGS I DONE--
--BUT I CAN'T FIND ANYONE--
--ANYONE TO HUH--HELP
DON'T.
DON'T TALK LIKE THAT. JUST HANG ON.
YOU'RE NOT A BAD PERSON. I'M GOING TO DIG YOU OUT AND YOU'LL BE FINE.
DO YOU HEAR ME?

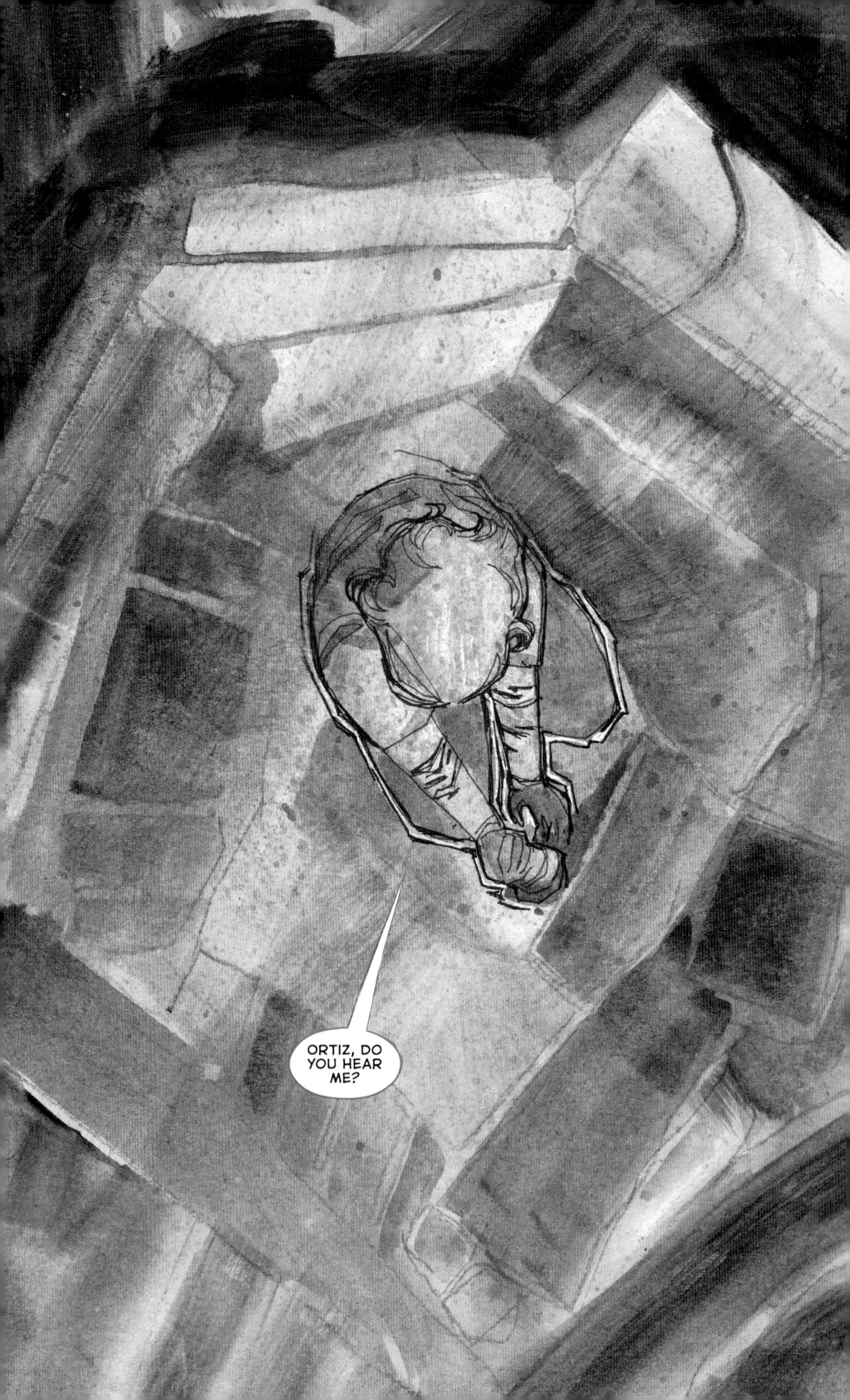
ORTIZ, DO YOU HEAR ME?

UNDERWINTER

THE QUEEN OF SPIRITS

PART FIVE

WHAT?
WHAT DID HE SAY TO YOU? YOUR NAME'S NOT CHRIS?
EMMA!
DON'T LISTEN TO HIM! DON'T WORRY ABOUT THAT!
CAN YOU SEE ANYTHING? CAN YOU SEE THE QUEEN OF SPIRITS?
...WHO ARE YOU?

I'M GOING IN, I--
I CAN'T HOLD ON...
I SEE SOMEONE.
SOMEONE INSIDE...
I DID RECOGNIZE YOU. BUT IT TOOK ME A WHILE TO FIGURE OUT FROM WHERE. YOU WORKED THAT BAR. THE SLIDE, WHERE THEY'D HAVE BANDS IN ALL THE TIME.
EMMA PLAYED THERE. SO DID I.
THAT'S WHERE WE'D SEEN YOU. THAT'S WHERE YOU SAW US.
ONCE I FIGURED THAT OUT I STARTED ON THE NEXT PART.
WHY WOULD YOU LIE AND SAY YOU DIDN'T KNOW US?

I SEE HER!
SHE'S IN HERE! SHE'S WAITING FOR US! I CAN SEE HER!
OH SHIT. HELP ME, I DON'T WANT TO GO UP THERE.
NO? WHY'S THAT?
TAKE MY HAND! JUST HELP ME FOR A MINUTE!
I'LL TELL YOU! I'LL TELL YOU WHAT YOU WANT TO KNOW!
YEAH?
SO YOU CAN BE FORGIVEN?

FUCK YOU.
I TELL YOU I SAW THE GUY WHO KNIFED ME?
USED TO SEE HIM AROUND THE SLIDE A LOT TOO. MAYBE YOU KNEW HIM.
PLEASE...
OH MY GOD.
YEAH, YOU'RE SCARED NOW.
I HOPE YOU DON'T GET IT OUT BEFORE YOU SEE HER.
YOU HEAR ME?
I HOPE SHE'S REAL AND YOU MISS YOUR CHANCE.

THERE YOU GO. GO ON IN.
NO. NO, I DON'T WANT TO--
She beckons

HELLO?

I HAVE PREPARED FOR THIS DAY FOR FIFTY YEARS.

There is a humming sound, a halfway human sound. Black shadow settles near the ground like heavy smoke, shot through with smoke, real smoke
Though nothing in here is exactly real. The silhouetted figures, featureless, darker than the night sky. He is half vanished already and the words rattle from him, dry and cold.
WHAT--
WHAT AM I SUPPOSED TO DO?
ARE YOU THE QUEEN OF SPIRITS?
There is another window far beyond them and it glows with light.
Or is it the window he just entered? Is he facing it now, from within the darkness? He has no sense of place here.
One of the figures beckons. One of them whispers his name. His actual name. A long, sibilant hiss.

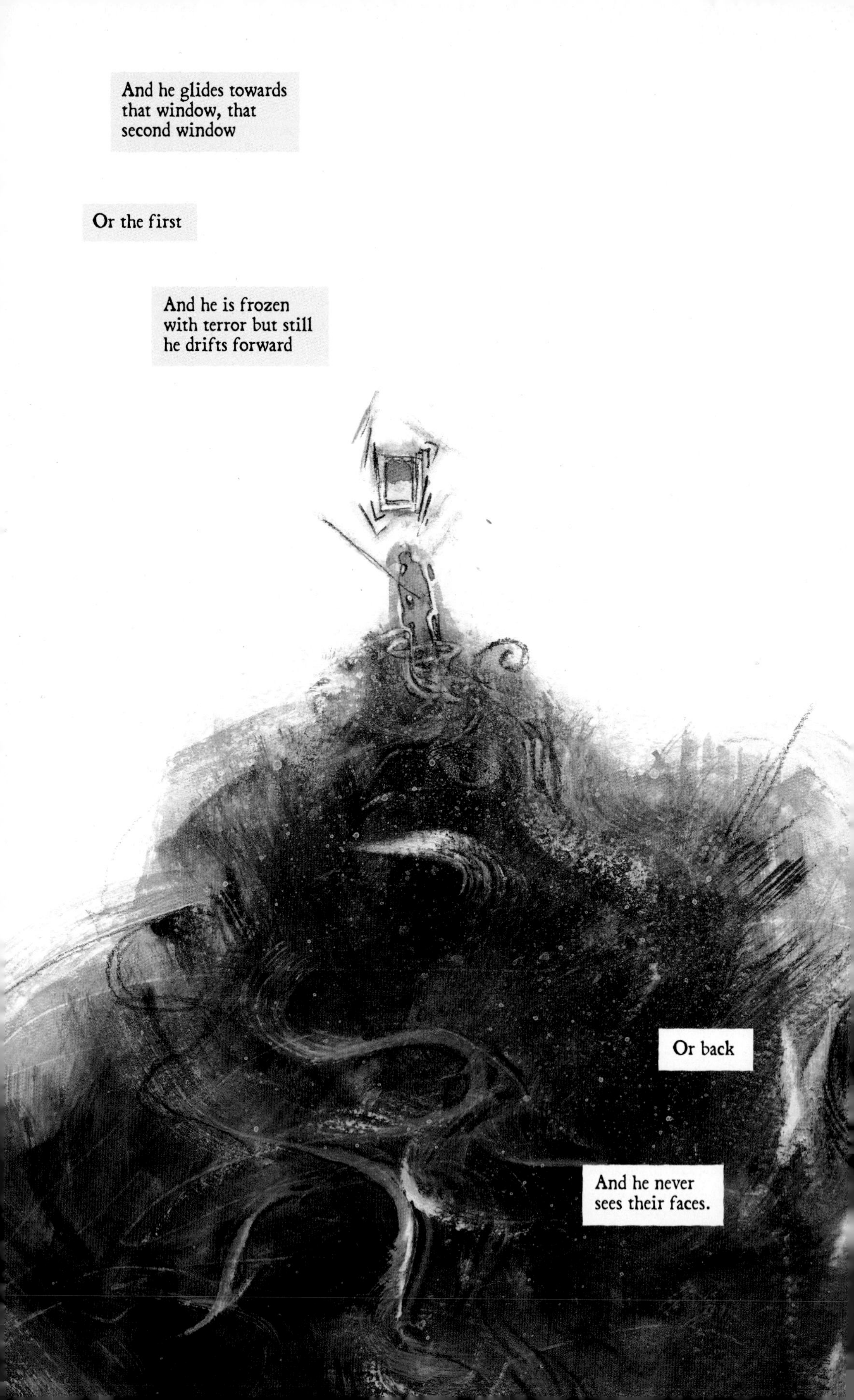
And he glides towards that window, that second window
Or the first
And he is frozen with terror but still he drifts forward
Or back
And he never sees their faces.

He weeps.
The light begins to fragment.
I SWORE I WOULD PAY ANY PRICE.
AND I HAVE PAID.
OH, HOW I HAVE PAID.

...DID IT WORK?

RING RING
HEY. YEAH, I TURNED IT OFF. YEAH, I'M THERE. I'M THERE.
I KNOW. I KNOW. TELL THE KIDS I LOVE THEM VERY MUCH. TELL THEM MOMMY'S GOING TO BE HOME VERY SOON.
YES. VERY SOON.
I'M DOING THE BEST I CAN.

END

September 7, 1971

They are here. They are among us. And their weapon is built into us. Murder and mayhem have been slipped into the human fabric for so long that people think it is our nature now. They have no idea. Every word we speak or write is distorted by them. Do you understand? We can never trust or fully comprehend any attempt to conventionally warn each other or organize ourselves. They are invisible. They are distortion. Even this text is warping my message. You will not be sufficiently prepared. I know it wasn't always like this. I've dreamed the time before. I dreamed it the day we passed behind the moon. I'm not the only one. But I think I might be the only one who's still alive, two years later.

September 7, 197

They are here. They are us. And their
weapon is Murder.

speak or write. Do you understand? We
can trust fully
convention
They are visible.
this text is my message. You will
be sufficiently prepared. I know it.

January 13, 1972

The Tower of Babel was a mistranslation. The original story is true. The original story can only be told in the original language. We still have it. It's the only language they can't touch. They want to wipe it out so that nothing remains but their truth. The one they've overlaid on us. The one that traps us.

I have met people who are trying to break their overlay. They scatter the distortion and reassemble it, to see if we can sneak actual truth through the remains. It might work. I hope it works. They fight on their own front. I respect them.

I have met people who have theories about how to draw and direct their attention with the original language. It's very risky but I'm told it works. I saw someone try it once and he did not survive the attempt. I don't know if the method ever works. But the theory is there.

We have our plan, our own plan. Even speaking it to one another means that we can't be sure we are all operating in concert. The enemy may be warping our attempts. Subtly or otherwise. This is the problem. We can't communicate. We

the any Scatter nature human alive only
weapon invisible one They original tower the
The sneak the the are overlay The never to
among hope sneak We reassemble original word
Mistranslation prepared people overlay the

We are one to hope people. The original sneak,
the overlay. Scatter the overlay.
The never nature, the original sneak.
Mistranslation weapon, among any tower. They
reassemble the human prepared the only alive
word invisible.

The overlay Mistranslation among human the
weapon invisible any original reassemble
nature people overlay to the only original alive
are tower one The the We sneak Scatter the the
word never prepared sneak They hope

the hope tower any The Scatter weapon
prepared nature They Mistranslation sneak
overlay The We are the one word invisible the
people original overlay human to reassemble
sneak never original the only among the alive
never can.

The weapon invisible

The hope tower

The never nature

The original sneak

The scatter language

Broken telephone

No two entries in this diary are written by the same person. It was passed to me today. I don't know what to say. Everyone who writes in this thing has seen them. That doesn't mean we understand. I don't understand anything. I tried to tell the guy who gave me this but he told me to write and then pass it on to the next person who sees them.

Maybe I'll tell about the time I saw them. I was watching my brother put together a sequencer, like a drum machine. I don't know what it's called. He's the one who was so into those things. He put it together and he tried it out. He pushed a button and it started to play. I was looking out the window, just sitting. It was raining. It started playing this sound like tinny drums and he was really happy and I sort of saw this THING looking in through the window and if you've seen one you know what I mean, it looks like partly a person but it doesn't look like anything and it's HUGE.

People in this book talking about fighting them and this is called a War Diary but I don't know what I'm supposed to do. Take this book and hand it to the next person I guess and try not to go crazy.

We are the tower. Every time one of us grows, they **m**ove to destroy **us**. It takes everything we have to stay al**i**ve and stay on **c**ourse. Don't give up. We're fighting. Each **i**n our own way. Do you under**s**tand? You know the original **language**. You've known it all your life. Everyone has their own ideas. Each of these entries is trying to get to you one way or another. But we can't just say it outright. It's clear that when we try, the entry is warped beyond comprehension.

Has it been one enemy all along, or have there been many? Do they hand the battle off to one another like we do?

You can't see me but you
know as soon as I'm
around
I fill every space I'm in
I travel very quickly
I can change how you
feel
I can make you move
without thought
What am I

You can't see me but you
know as soon as I'm
around
I fill every space I'm in
I travel very quickly
I can change how you
feel
I can make you move
without thought
What am I

You can't see me but you
know as soon as I'm
around
I fill every space I'm in
I travel very quickly
I can change how you
feel
I can make you move
without thought
What am I

You can't see me but you
know as soon as I'm
around
I fill every space I'm in
I travel very quickly
I can change how you
feel
I can make you move
without thought
What am I

You can't see me but you
know as soon as I'm
around
I fill every space I'm in
I travel very quickly
I can change how you
feel
I can make you move
without thought
What am I

I heard about a plan. It costs a lot. Maybe too much. I can't think about it, it hurts to even think it. Ten thousand souls. Ten thousand souls to form a lens and through that lens we will all be able to see. Is it worth it? Even when we can see, what can we do? No, if we can see, we can fight back. We won't be ignored any more. We won't sound crazy. Not when we can point and say there they are there it is.

It will take years. Decades. Spinning a web to bring them all in, to catch them and then to shape them. The plan itself is awful, so awful. Even to think it. Even to say it and say we need to pick a place and we need to start. When do we start. Even to choose a date.

December 31, 1995

Philadelphia. Today.

I had a plan. It cost a lot. too much.
I hurt Ten thousand souls.

all Even
? No .
no . No
.

I w a s b a
d
awful,
sa d

September 2, 2008

It's not over. The records are distorted. They want you to believe we've lost and can't win. Think carefully. Look around. What's happening to the people who fight on our side? They're still disappearing. They're still being driven mad and tearing themselves apart and drugging drinking hollowed out eating not eating themselves to death. Why? Because it's not over. The plan is on. They haven't erased Philadelphia from our journals. Why?

October 21 2018

Hello Philadelphia

Are you ready to rock

I said

Are you ready to rock

Well all right then

HIT

IT

HIT

IT

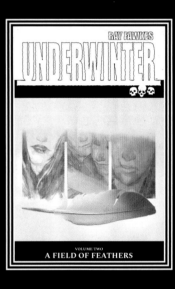